AF250184

Milly:

My Life as a Labradoodle
… in Five Short Dog Tales

ROBERT BELENKY

CONTENTS

Acknowledgments vii

Little Arf and Nanny 1

The Snarf-Ball Saga 9

Let Lying Dogs Sleep...23

Problematic Squirrels 31

The Dog Star 43

Afterword: Where Truth Lies...............................49

ACKNOWLEDGMENTS

To my resolutely supportive family, to all the children I have known, and to dogs and dog lovers everywhere.

With special thanks to Sophie Bodner and Bob Franzoni of CATV8, White River Junction, Vermont.

And Shiloh Savage: Milly, Squirt, and I really *love* to hear you read dog tales!

Little Arf and Nanny

Although Milly lived a perfectly good and happy life with her adoptive parents, Mother Mary and Capt'n Bob, she dwelled on the fact that she began life as an orphan and deep down inside still thinks of herself as one. Hers is a sad story. She sheds silent tears when she thinks about it.

Here she tells the tale in her own words as translated by her father, Capt'n Bob, from the original language consisting of yips, barks, body wiggles, and tail wags:

"I was born in Claudia's house. Claudia was a woman who adored dogs. She bred us for a living and ran a nice little kennel in her house, mostly in the living room.

"Claudia had many young grandchildren. Some lived with her, and some just dropped by from time to time to visit. The children loved to play with dogs, especially with us, the puppies. We in turn loved the children.

"I was the third youngest of a litter of twelve. My mother, whose name was Nanny, was a black Labrador Retriever. Her body was always warm, she produced the most delicious milk, and best of all, she exuded a heavenly scent that I still recall in my dreams. My brothers, sisters, and I loved her with all our hearts.

"We all slept a lot in those days, but every now and then we would wake up, tussle with each other a bit, then slide over to Mom for a nourishing meal, all we could drink. It was a glorious life, a heavenly life. We loved our mom, our mom loved us, and we loved each other. What could be better than that?

"Claudia told us that we had a father, a big tan standard poodle. He lived in a cage out in the yard. Other dogs told me that he was a fine fellow. I think I met him, but frankly, I don't remember him at all.

"Things went along very well for days in this way, maybe even weeks. But suddenly it all changed. We lost our paradise. It started when I was sucking at my favorite teat, gulping down my customary helping of Mom's warm, intoxicating milk, when from out of the blue, Mommy screamed, 'Yeeowch!'

"'Mommy,' I cried. 'Mommy dearest, what in the world is the matter?'

"'It's your miserable, sharp, stupid little teeth, Arf!" (that was my name then). 'You are a rotten little monster,' she growled. 'If you want to get fed by me, go see a dentist! Get those miserable teeth yanked!'

"I had no idea what she was talking about. In the first place, I didn't know what a dentist was. I didn't even know what teeth were. All I knew was that my darling mother was mad at me. As far as I knew, there was no reason for it. I was sure I had done nothing wrong.

"I crawled away from her, sobbing, and stumbled over to join my brothers and sisters. They all told pretty much the same story.

"'Why has our saintly mother suddenly gone bad?' we asked each other.

"'She's out of her mind,' Rufus exclaimed.

"'However shall we eat?' Belle sobbed.

"'We shall starve!' we cried, all of us at once.

"Just then Madame Claudia entered our den. She carried a bunch of little glass bottles with her. Each had warm cow's milk inside and a rubber nipple at the end. She gently picked us up one at a time and allowed us to drink our fill. That made us feel better, but before falling asleep again, we cried because we missed our warm, sweet-smelling mommy.

"Somehow we survived, but we were left feeling miserable.

"In the next few days, Mme Claudia brought a series of human visitors to our den. They looked us over, picked up one or two of us at a time, and said something to Mme Claudia that we could not understand.

"Soon my brothers and sisters began to disappear, one by one. None of us were old enough to run away. So ... what could have happened? Where could the puppies have gone? Had people eaten them? Had they wandered off? Were they lost? Were they hungry?

Those of us who remained were very, very worried, but no one could even imagine an answer to any of our questions.

"Then one day—I remember it well—Mother Mary and Capt'n Bob showed up at Mme Claudia's. I didn't know them, but they seemed nice enough. Mary picked me up, placed me on her lap, and stroked my fur. I really liked that and decided right away that she was a good person. Capt'n Bob seemed okay, too, but he didn't do much except talk to Claudia.

"'This is your new mom,' Claudia explained, referring to Mary. 'And this is your new dad,' she added, pointing to Capt'n Bob.

"I fell asleep soon after that feeling much better than I had, but I was still a bit worried. What was to become of me?

"You know the rest. Mother Mary and Capt'n Bob turned out to be loving adoptive parents, and I led a good life with them. All went very well for me—very well, that is, until one day when something happened that made me sad once again.

"Six months went by. I was by then a remarkably good-looking, half-grown, highly-educated, and beautifully groomed lady dog. Because Mary and Bob planned to go somewhere for a few days, a backward sort of place that does not allow dogs, they decided to have me stay for a while at Claudia's, where they thought I would be happy since that had been my puppyhood home. Little did they know.

"Imagine my delight and surprise when I caught sight of my sainted mother in the play yard.

"I trembled with excitement when Mme Claudia picked me up and brought me to the fence, opened the gate, and tossed me inside.

"'Mommy!' I barked. 'Mommy dearest! How wonderful to be with you again.'

"She gave me an odd look. 'Who are you?' she growled impatiently.

"'It's me,' I said, 'your favorite daughter. You must remember me. My name was Arf then. It is Milly now.'

"'I never saw you in my long life,' she growled again, visibly irritated.

"Tears came to my eyes. 'I took the third teat from the right of your tail,' I mumbled sadly. 'You surely must remember. How, how, how could you have forgotten me?' I wailed, hot tears streaming down the fur of my cheeks.

"'Oh my God!' Mom howled in sudden terror. 'It has all come back to me now! You are the one I called 'Snagletooth.' You chomped so hard on my teat that I had to see the vet.

"'Help! Help!' she barked. 'Get this miserable little monster out of here! At once! At once, I tell you! At once.'

"Mme Claudia arrived seconds later, scooped me up, and placed me in the living room cage.

"That was the worst moment of my life. I cried and cried but eventually fell asleep shivering and alone when I dreamed the most terrible dreams.

"Mary and Bob returned the next morning and took me home. I was so very happy to see them. I tried to explain what had happened, but frankly, they did not seem interested. And besides, they are not very good at understanding dog talk. On the other hand, they did give me my favorite dog chow plus leftover chicken soup. I then fell fast asleep, this time to my usual pleasant dreams.

"And that is my story. I never saw my mother again. But from then on, I had a passionate interest in helping abandoned dogs and children find a home where they are taken care of and properly loved. It doesn't need to be with their natural parents. Foster or adoptive parents will do just as well … especially if the chicken soup is warm, is well prepared, and reeks of a savory scent."

The Snarf-Ball Saga

"I love, love, love to play tennis," said Milly.

"That's preposterous," I said. "Dogs can't possibly play tennis."

"Well, I can," Milly said.

I could see that we had a misunderstanding. "Remind me: exactly how do you play this game you call tennis," I asked.

"Simple," she said. "Dad, you toss me the tennis ball. I catch it, and I spend the afternoon chomping on it."

Yes, we certainly had a misunderstanding—a bad one.

To clear things up, I shall now tell you everything I know about this, the full and honest story.

When Milly was a baby, no one would have guessed that there was anything special about her. She was tiny, black, and furry. She slept a great deal and played mostly by chasing leaves in the warm months and snowflakes in winter. She was a happy, fun-loving animal who led a good life with her parents, Mary and myself, Capt'n Bob. We adopted her when she was eight weeks old.

Milly never got into fights with other dogs and never bit anyone, neither canine nor human, except once when she was very young and had extremely sharp teeth. In a playful mood and meaning no harm, she chomped on a friend's finger, drawing blood.

The woman was rushed to the hospital, where she received two stitches. Milly immediately apologized.

It was an embarrassing moment, even more so as she grew older and learned good manners. She then pledged to devote her life to peace and love.

The woman forgave Milly immediately, but the memory stayed with the poor dog. She never forgave herself.

And so Milly grew up to be a peacemaker. When other dogs got into fights, she stood aside and barking calmly, tried to convince them to make friends and play a fast game of chase with each other instead. That usually worked, especially when Milly was there to help them deal with any other problems that might come up.

Most dogs really respected Milly and always did the right thing when they knew she was watching … although frankly not so much when she left the scene. In any case, it was clear that she was a very fair-minded animal and an excellent influence on everyone around her. It is hard to say exactly how that came about. She was just that kind of dog.

Milly, by the way, especially loved children, human as well as dog children. She liked to bark merrily and play you can't catch me with them.

Children could tell right away that she was an extremely good dog and were never afraid of her. Mothers and fathers trusted her, too.

But Milly, like all of us, had her problems that she did not wish to talk about. One of these was particularly disturbing to tennis players in Hanover, New Hampshire. It was whispered that Milly was in the habit of stealing tennis balls.

Not such a bad thing, you say? Maybe not, but it did bother people and made her something less than a perfect dog in their eyes. This upset her. "I do *not* steal tennis balls," she insisted more than once, sometimes tearfully. "I am a *good* dog, indeed a *perfect* dog."

"Then why is it said that you steal tennis balls?" I asked.

"It is a misunderstanding," she said.

"Please explain yourself," I said.

"You can't steal what is yours," she said. "It's very simple. Any dog can tell you that. Dogs understand these things. But people, to tell the truth, have oatmeal for brains. You have to explain everything over and over to them."

"You argue like a lawyer," I said.

"What is a lawyer?" Milly asked.

"A lawyer—an elegant name for which is attorney— is someone who goes to college to study the practice of arguing. Some become lawyers to become rich and famous, but most do so to make the world a fairer place."

"Wow!" Milly said. "That's for me! I shall be a lawyer so people will be fair to me, thus making the world a fairer place one dog at a time.

"Send me to law school, Dad. *Please!*"

"Nonsense," I said. "Dogs cannot be lawyers. Only people can be lawyers."

"That is so *unfair!*" Milly howled.

"Forget it," she growled, her head hanging low. "I don't need you or Mom. I will go to law school anyway. On my own!"

That night when Mary, my wife, and I were sound asleep, Milly slipped out of the house and ran all the way to the Vermont Law School, where she stayed three years. She sent us an e-mail soon after she left, in which she explained what she had done and assured us that she would be back as soon as she learned enough about the law to defend herself.

Every week after that, we received an e-mail from her in which she let us know that she was happy and in good health had many dog and people friends and was learning a lot.

One evening we heard a scratching at the front door. We opened it, and there was Milly, a diploma in her teeth and a square black hat perched on her head with a red ribbon hanging down.

"I am now an attorney," she explained, "America's first girl dog to become one."

"Congratulations!" Mary and I shouted together joyously. We were so happy to see her! We treated her to her favorite dog crunchies with a beef bone on top plus a big bowl of water. She gobbled down the crunchies and gulped down the water, smacking her lips when she finished. She then proceeded to chomp on the bone.

We had lots of questions, but Milly had a long day and was tired. She stretched, yawned, curled up on the sofa, and fell asleep.

Before breakfast the next morning, Milly and I took a stroll in the park across the way. I brought along a tennis ball. When we reached the grassy area, I tossed the ball as high as I could. Milly ran after it, leaped, and caught it on the first bounce. She then took it to her favorite spot under an old oak tree and proceeded to chomp on it.

Just then a big German shepherd ran up to her. He wore a sparkling badge on his collar. "Where did you get that tennis ball?" he asked in a gruff tone of voice.

"My dad, Capt'n Bob, threw it to me."

"Are you Milly, the famous tennis-ball-stealing dog?"

"I am Milly, but I *don't* steal tennis balls."

"A likely story," the German shepherd growled, showing his teeth.

"She tells you the truth, sir," I said. "I did throw that ball to her."

"Sorry," he growled again. "We have orders to look out for this Milly character, arrest her, and bring her to court. She has a very bad reputation."

"Don't worry, Dad," Milly said. "I can handle this. I am an attorney now."

Two days later, the German shepherd brought Milly to the judge, a fast-talking miniature schnauzer with a long beard and a high, squeaky voice.

Milly was not frightened.

"Well," the judge said in a high-pitched bark, "did you steal that tennis ball or did you not?"

"I did not, Your Honor," Milly said firmly.

"Tell me your side of the story then, miss," said the judge.

"I have frequently been accused, sir—in the complete absence of proof—of stealing tennis balls. Some dogs spread that rumor; so do some people.

"But I am *not* a thief. I do *not* steal. To steal is to take something that does not belong to you. I have never done that, and I never will. Each and every tennis ball I own is mine. And I shall prove it to you right now.

"First, allow me to admit that I do in fact adore tennis balls, the real ones that are white and fuzzy and fit neatly in my mouth. Their fuzziness tickles my tongue when I chomp on them. Oh, it is such a happy sensation! Have you tried it, sir? Do so. You will then know what I mean. Even better are the orange rubbery ones that have the texture of uncooked chicken. They have no taste at all, but the sensation on the tongue is heavenly. This type of ball is not actually used to play tennis. It was invented to be given to dog tennis ball lovers like me.

"I collect both kinds of balls, sir, and I am proud to say that in my collection today there are hundreds, perhaps half of the first kind and a quarter, the second.

"You may wonder how I obtained them. I shall tell you: Most were thrown to me. I found the rest."

"Who threw them?" the judge asked.

"My dad, Capt'n Bob. He has a pink plastic stick with a place for a ball at the end of it. He puts the ball there, reaches back, and gives it a heave. The ball flies through the air and lands way far away. I leap after it and am usually able to grab it in the air on no more than one bounce. I then chomp on it.

"Sometimes I tease my dad. I bring the ball to him and drop it at his feet. He reaches down to grab it, intending to heave it again. But just as his hand is close, I snarf it up with my teeth and dance away, laughing myself silly. Later I add the ball to my collection.

I do this not to annoy or disrespect the Capt'n but because it's funny. Cracks me up every time. Dad gets annoyed but is usually able to take the joke pretty well. He knows that I *never* do anything out of meanness."

"Do you enjoy this foolish and fun-loving game?" the schnauzer judge asked.

"Oh, yes indeed sir! It is great, great fun! I do love that game! Love it! Love it! Love it."

"And what do you call this game of yours?" the pure-bred judge wondered peering over his glasses.

"'Tennis,' sir. It is my favorite sport. I don't like to boast, your honor, but I am a star. In any case, that is how the tennis balls got to be mine. They are gifts, you see, sir, mostly from Capt'n Bob."

"But," said the judge, "doesn't Capt'n Bob, your dear father, expect that you will return the ball to him when you are done chomping on it?"

"No, your honor. It is the same with bones. When a beef bone is thrown to me, I naturally assume that it is mine to chomp on for as long as I wish. It would not so much as enter my mind that it might belong to someone else. How could it possibly?

"A badly brought up dog may attempt to steal such a bone from me, but my fearsome growl usually puts an end to any such nonsense.

"In conclusion: I say that if a ball is thrown to someone, whether dog or person, it becomes a gift, fair and square. It is then his or hers to chomp on. That is how the world works.

"Therefore, it should be clear to everyone that I am indeed a good dog. Some might say a *very* good dog."

"Yes. You are obviously a highly moral animal," the judge said, "a most remarkably honest dog.

In conclusion, we find that you are innocent. It is equally evident that you do not steal tennis balls.

"The court also notes," he added, "that you have argued your case very well indeed."

"Thank you for your understanding, Your Honor. I argued well only because I am an attorney," Milly said modestly.

"Case dismissed. You may return home now."

Milly greeted the just verdict with a series of yips that accompanied a rapid wagging of her tail and a series of six runs—and twice as many leaps—around the courtroom. The judge descended from his chair and joined her for one run and one leap—but only one of each. In deference to his position, he was obliged to remain dignified.

When we arrived home, I said. "Milly, you won, but let's face it: you do in fact steal tennis balls. Everybody knows it. And what's more, you don't actually play tennis. You play a goofy 'snarf-ball' game and make up the rules as you go along."

"Grrrr!" said Milly. "But hey, Dad! It's time for our afternoon walk. Let's get *out* of here!"

"Oh, Dad?" Milly yipped cheerily as we headed out the door.

"Yes, Milly dear?"

"Don't forget to bring along a bunch of my very best tennis balls."

"Grrrr!" I said.

Questions for the Intelligent Reader

1. Does Milly *really* steal tennis balls?

2. If she does, can she still be a good dog?

3. What makes a dog good?

4. What makes a dog bad?

5. Was the judge's decision influenced by Milly's great beauty and charm?

6. If you needed a lawyer, would you or would you not hire Milly? Why/why not?

Let Lying Dogs Sleep

As you are no doubt aware, I am Milly—the famous Milly. I was named after a comic strip from the 1940s, "Silly Milly." It ran in the old *New York Post* ages ago, long before it became, as my dad, Capt'n Bob, says, "a conservative rag." I know it isn't dignified to be named after a comic strip, but I think it's funny to be known as "Silly."

Dad and I have political disagreements. The other day he mumbled, "The Republican Party has gone to the dogs."

"Woof!" I said. "Where do I sign up?"

He gave me a pitying look that really hurt my feelings.

I am a dark brown Labradoodle and proud of it. Some people think I am black, but I am not. I am dark brown. I am also very clever, beauiful and all told, a lovely animal. Capt'n Bob writes short stories about me that are mostly lies or exaggerations at best.

I shall now tell you in my own words the full and honest truth about myself and the life I lead.

Mine is a usual dog tale. My adoptive mother, Mary, and my adoptive dad, Bob—whom I like to call "Capt'n Bob" because he likes to paddle his kayak— wake up each morning early. I hear them mumble that it's six thirty or seven or some such. I myself can't read clocks, but I know it's morning when my stomach aches for breakfast.

By the time I stretch and yawn and wander half awake into the kitchen for my customary kibbles, it's around nine. My mom, Mother Mary, often says, "Milly is the only dog I know who sleeps in."

Yes, I do like to sleep in—usually on the rug but often on my favorite chair, the one that I share with Mother Mary.

Anyway, my parents eventually stumble by me on their way to the bathroom. They pat me on the head and belly. I wag my tail in return.

We live in a retirement community for old people, but most of the dogs here are young like me. All told, it is a good life—lots of fun. I am very popular with everyone—staff, residents, dogs, and visitors, no matter their age or species.

I have many interests, and I am good at many things. I especially like to play tennis. I also love to dance and, incidentally, I am told that I am a great dancer. I bark a lot and wag my tail, especially when I tell jokes to amuse my dog friends.

And when I have nothing better to do, I curl up and listen to conversations—people conversations and dog conversations. I listen to cat conversations, too, when I have the opportunity.

I enjoy going out for walks with the Capt'n—way into the woods or around an open field. Either is fine with me. I dutifully pee and then poop at that time. I often meet dog friends. We chase each other and exchange gossip.

It is a great life.

I especially love to sleep and to sleep, perchance to dream. Dreaming indeed is my favorite entertainment. I had an interesting dream last night, by the way. Let me tell you about it.

There I was in a lively kennel. My parents were off somewhere for a few days. I wasn't worried. They have done that before and always come back.

I was having a fine time in the yard chasing a bunch of quick-witted young dogs. Around and around and around we went until we collapsed all in a heap, gasping and grunting in the happiest way. As we lay there, we got to talking. As you know, we dogs don't talk with our voices the way people do. We just sort of think, and somehow our thoughts land right in the other animal's head. It's hard to explain, but that's how it works.

Anyway, we got into a discussion of pets. One of the dogs, a cute young mutt named Nefertiti, said that she longs to have a frog of her own, one that she can hold between her front paws and gaze at lovingly.

King Kong, a fearsome-looking English bulldog, grunted his opinion that the best pet for any animal is a monkey, preferably the Capuchin kind.

Picking up on that theme, Lori, a hairless Chihuahua, explained her theory that the very best pet for clever dogs like us is the human being, especially the young human child. "They are remarkably intelligent," she said, "and very playful as well as imaginative. Plus they don't bite. They are very kindly, too, at least that's my experience."

Well, I don't know. I prefer old people. I told the group that my own parents are elderly. Although they are human beings and obviously way over the hill, as one says, they are lively enough for my needs. In addition, they are generous and feed me well. I said that I would vote for kindly old people as pets if it came to that.

On the other hand, I am a very proud dog and famous everywhere for my open mindedness, so I made a point of taking Lori's opinion into serious consideration.

Just then a gaggle of human children came along, all of them merry and giggly.

"Ah," said Lori, "here come my pets now. You will see what I mean."

We had a lovely time, all of us together. The children chased us, and we chased them. I barked repeatedly at a little girl. I made sure that I was not scary but hilariously funny instead. I danced and she laughed.

"You can't catch me!" I yelled in dog language, which she seemed to understand without difficulty. Then she tore after me, and I tore after her. Neither of us caught the other, but we didn't care.

Eventually everybody sank down together on the grass, grown-up dogs and human puppies all in one big pile.

Yes, I thought. *I shall definitely get myself a people-puppy for a pet.* "But how to find one?" I asked Lori.

"In a store," she said. "A pet store. If you want to buy a pet, you must go to a pet store … naturally."

"Of course," I mumbled, pretending I knew all about such things.

I then found myself trotting down the main street of a town that resembled Lebanon, New Hampshire. I spotted a barbershop and a bank, a sporting goods store, a restaurant, and a ladies' clothing shop. But unfortunately, no pet shop.

I was about to give up when Elizabeth, a classy black Lab—who reminded me of my dear, long lost mother—trotted along on a leash, on the other end of which was a geeky human boy by the name of George.

We wagged our tails, Elizabeth and I, as George grinned in a friendly, personable way. The two of them paused for a moment; then Elizabeth and I, out of mutual respect, sniffed each other's hindquarters.

"Do you know where I can find a pet store?" I asked Elizabeth.

"What kind of pet are you looking for?" George wanted to know.

"A human puppy," I explained.

The two of them looked at me as if I were not very intelligent. "You don't get people puppies in a pet store!" George explained, laughing.

"No." Elizabeth grinned. "You get them in a place called a *school*. That's what schools are for."

"Of course," I lied. "I knew that."

"There happens to be a school right down the street," Elizabeth continued. "Why don't you trot over there and see if they have any pretty people puppies on sale?"

That sounded like very good advice, so that was just what I did.

When I arrived at the schoolhouse door …

[Here we ask children viewers to send us their recommendation for continuing or ending the story. What do you say, kids?]

Problematic Squirrels

Milly gets along with just about everybody and anybody, animal or human. She makes friends very easily. She has a great many individuals who not only love but also respect her, people as well as dogs, and she loves and respects them in return.

In addition, unusual for a dog of her class and position, she has a number of interesting cat acquaintances, some of whom she counts among her closest friends and in whom she can confide her innermost thoughts.

Milly is an enlightened canine. She is generous with her time and completely trusting as well as trustful. Everyone who knows her believes in her. And she believes in them.

She extends her positive attitude beyond individuals to important political issues. She is a charter member, for example, of the Hanover, New Hampshire, "Black

Dog" Society and has initiated the "Drop the Leash" movement, which, I am told, is catching on nationally.

Milly is therefore unusually worldly for a local animal with little experience in the big world.

A final example: One of her very best friends is a certain Squirt. Squirt happens to be a white dog, but that does not bother Milly at all. In fact, she seems to enjoy being seen in public with him. His presence makes clear to everyone that she is a fair animal, entirely without prejudice.

Milly is therefore remarkable in every respect. Almost.

The single exception to what I have related: Milly does not appreciate squirrels.

"Squirrels?" I asked. "What's the matter with squirrels?"

"Unfortunately," she said, "I have never met a squirrel I could trust, none that was worth the time of day. Squirrels are born cheats, sneaks, and busybodies— every last one of them."

"I am surprised at you, Milly, shocked indeed as well as disappointed. Why do you come up with such terrible, prejudiced nonsense?"

"You don't *know* squirrels," she snapped back. "I do. Believe me, they are a primitive, entirely dishonest species. What's more, they want to take over our forest.

"They also talk in stupid, squeaky sentences that nobody can understand: *eeech, eeech, eeech.* No normal animal talks like that. Why can't they bark like decent dogs?

"Plus, they hop. They don't gallop like a self-respecting animal. They hop, hop, hop. It is disgusting to watch.

"And they are sneaky. You come up to them for a friendly sniff of the back side and, *zip!* They disappear up the nearest tree.

"Finally—they steal acorns from trees and the forest floor—not that I especially like acorns. It's the principle of the thing.

"I tell you: They are terrorists and a dangerous threat to our way of life."

With that, she was off. "I have a meeting of the Black Dog Society," she explained. "We are discussing the squirrel threat this very night."

Her words hit me hard. This was not the fair-minded, peace-loving Milly I knew. Who was this mad dog? Where had we as parents failed?

"Wait, Milly," I shouted after her. "We've *got* to talk this over!"

"Some other time," she yelled back. "I can't be late. I am also giving a paper on the evils of leash laws."

The next day I ran into Milly in Storrs Pond Park. She no longer lives with us, by the way. She is a grownup now and has a lovely den for herself in a nearby stable.

Mary and I haven't yet had a chance to visit her. But Milly has always liked being around horses, and horses do tend to love and respect her. I'm sure it's okay.

I asked her how she could afford such fine lodgings. "Oh, I have a very good job," she explained with visible pride. "Police work."

"What do you do?"

"I mind the henhouse. The guard before me was a red fox on an all-bird diet. He stuffed himself, and they fired him."

Just then a tiny gray squirrel with a huge, bushy tail scampered by.

Milly leaped to her feet and scrambled after it. But the squirrel merely stuck its tongue out as if to say, "*Nyeh, nyeh*, you can't catch me!" Then it scrambled up a leafy maple tree and was gone.

Milly galloped after it but to no avail. She even tried to climb the tree, but being vain, she was embarrassed by how foolish she thought she looked. She gave up and returned, growling, to where I sat.

"Horrible, horrible little pests," she grumbled. "We should send them back to where they came from."

"Calm down, Milly," I said. "What harm does a little squirrel do? Why not live and let live?"

"There you go again," Milly growled. "You are a *namby-pamby* do-gooder. I'll *tell* you what harm they do: they steal acorns. That's what they do."

"Big deal," I said. "I didn't know you like acorns."

"I don't," Milly admitted. "It's the principle of the thing."

Just then a second squirrel came loping across the lawn, this time a young, pretty one.

"Monster!" Milly screamed and scooted after the terrified rodent.

The poor squirrel scrambled up the trunk of a nearby maple tree and disappeared in its uppermost branches.

Milly tried to follow but got no further than bumping her head on the trunk just above the ground, far below its lowest branches.

Then she got her foot stuck in a rabbit hole.

"Curses!" Milly screamed as she limped back to me. "We *must* put a stop to this nonsense! At once! At once, I tell you! At once!"

"How will you manage that?" I asked.

"I shall gather all of the local dogs together, and we will build a wall of stones and boulders all around the forest. No squirrel will be allowed through unless he or she takes the no-tree-climbing oath that I shall compose as soon as I return home. And … I will make the squirrels *pay* for it!"

Just then, a cheerful chipmunk scurried by, squeaked a squeaky, "Hi" to us, then scooted over a log and disappeared in the underbrush.

Milly leaped after it, but it ran very fast. Poor Milly was soon out of breath and breathing heavily. She did not pay attention to where she was going and plunged head first into a hedge of thorns and brambles.

She came limping back.

"And *chipmunks*," she growled, "are also *evil*! I *despise* them, too! *Utterly*!

"Well," I said. "Good luck on your project, Milly, foolish though it is."

As we parted, a graceful young deer stood alert and alone on a hillock no more than twenty yards away. She observed us carefully.

With an impulsive leap, Milly raced toward the deer, who provocatively shouted, *"See you later, Dogface!"* as it disappeared into the forest.

Milly limped back, huffing and puffing.

"Arrrrrgh!" she moaned. "You see what I mean? Look what it has come to: the lawn, the fields, the hills, and the forest are no longer part of the dog community. They have fallen into the hands of uncivilized strangers who have never so much as passed the time over a bone or a dog biscuit.

"They do not respect our customs. They do not speak either the dog or the people languages. They stick to themselves. They are up to no good.

"Yes, something must be done. It is time for our community to rise up and ... *go to the dogs!"*

We finally parted. I left, concerned about Milly, who had always been a most friendly of beasts, open to all creatures, whatever the species.

What had become of her?

That evening the neighborhood dogs gathered in Milly's stable. George, a splendid, gray-black, long-haired mutt, rose to open the meeting.

"Bitches and studs," he began. "Our respected founder, Milly, has asked us to come together to discuss a critical problem that affects our entire community. I therefore turn the meeting over to Milly."

[Thunderous barks and howls]

Milly wagged her tail in a dignified manner, rose, came forward, and took the microphone.

"Friends," she began, "as we have all noticed, our fields and forests have been overrun by hordes of foreign animals, squirrels, chipmunks, deer, and heaven knows what else. Is there no room left for traditional, old-fashioned, honest dogs?"

Shouts came from the audience. "Kick the foreigners out! Arrest them! Bite them!"

"I have a plan," Milly, hushing the crowd, continued. "We shall build a giant wall around our fields and forest. It will be so strong and so high that nobody will be able to climb it. And we shall make the squirrels pay for it in *acorns!*"

Cheers rang out from the crowd. "Yes! Yes! A wall! A wall! Yes! And pay for it in *acorns!*"

Milly raised her right front paw, and the crowd went silent. Then she continued, her voice rising: "And at long last, our entire community shall *go to the dogs*!"

[Prolonged barks, howls, and yips.]

After the meeting, everyone congratulated Milly on her inspiring talk and brilliant plan. Milly received the compliments graciously, politely sniffing each rear end in turn.

Later, on her way home, Milly happened upon a feeble old squirrel who hobbled across her path. He carried a big load of acorns in his mouth.

Suddenly he tripped, and the nuts spilled all over the path.

Although not disposed to socialize with squirrels, Milly remained in some respects a kindly animal despite everything.

Without a moment's thought, she rushed to his side. She helped him get up and proceeded to assist him in gathering the nuts, which she placed in a neat pile beside him.

"Thank you so much, miss," he said, breathing heavily as she guided him to a log, where he sat for a while to collect himself.

"I have a problem," Milly confessed. "I simply cannot help but be helpful. It is, unfortunately, in my nature."

"Please come to my nest," the old squirrel replied. "You will meet my lovely wife. Then the three of us can chat and drink a bit of fermented pine sap together."

"Thank you," Milly said. "I think I will. I have never visited a squirrel's nest before. It might prove an interesting experience."

Using a combination of vines, stones, twigs, and nut shells, the old squirrel helped Milly climb the chestnut tree, where, high in its branches, lay his home. His wife met them at the door.

"Where have you *been*, my dear?" she asked. "I was *so* worried! And who is this with you? A dog! My heavens, *a dog!* I do hope she did you no harm."

The old squirrel then told his wife the entire story. As to his canine companion, he added, "This is Milly, a highly moral dog who is my trusted friend and a friend to all squirrels everywhere."

Milly wagged her tail.

The Dog Star

Editor's note: This is a story about Milly. But it is not the Milly you know. It is her Grandma Milly, after whom our Milly was named. So please don't worry. Our Milly is still young. In February she will be only six. She still has a long, long way to go.

Got it? Okay. On to the story …

Grandma Milly is old now. She lives in a kennel down the road, where she has many friends. She spends her time sleeping for the most part, but when her nieces and nephews and various other friends and puppies visit, she likes to tell them about what the world was like when she was young.

The young animals' favorite story is the one Grandma Milly calls "The Dog Star." It goes like this.

****

When we were puppies, my friends and I had lots of fun. We would chase each other and play snarf-ball. We would swim and chase ducks all summer long, stuff ourselves on kibble, chicken soup, and beef bones, and then drift off to sleep together in one big heap.

For a special treat, we loved to attend concerts. The group we liked best was Harlan Wolf and His Wolverine Brothers and Sisters. These were cousins of ours whom we greatly admired.

Late at night once every month when the moon was full, Harlan and the Wolverines would assemble on the very top of Bald Mountain and sing to the moon. They had deep, rich voices. It was so beautiful.

On those nights, my friends and I would sneak out of our houses after everyone was asleep and dance down the dirt road together, chasing each other, giggling and singing.

Our families never knew.

When we reached the concert, we found places to sit with all the other dogs and foxes and wolves as well, everyone deeply moved and carried away by the music. Sometimes we and the foxes sang along with the wolves. But they had more enchanting howls than any of us, and so out of respect, we mostly wagged our tails in time to their magical music, and when we sang at all, we did our best to keep our voices low so as not to disturb the magic of the evening.

When midnight came near, a few of us began to dance. Soon the whole mountaintop was filled with dogs and foxes dancing to the song of the wolves. Thinking of it now brings tears of joy to my eye.

As I grew older, it occurred to me to wonder why Harlan and his wolverines came to sing to the moon in the first place. Was it because the moon is so beautiful or was the singing part of a religious ceremony of some sort? Is the moon sacred, a place of worship? Does a god live in the moon who hears the joyful but sometimes mournful songs of my wonderful cousins, the wolves?

One night I screwed up my courage and put the question to Harlan.

"No, no, no," Harlan said. "It's not like that at all, not at all. We only sing to ask the moon as respectfully as we can to please get out of our way."

"What?" I said.

"So that we can see the Dog Star more clearly, so that the moon does not hide it," he explained.

"The Dog Star?" I said.

"Yes," he said. "The real name is Sirius. It is the brightest star in the night sky. It is where all dogs, foxes and wolves go when they die. My ancestors are up there waiting for me. Someday I shall join them."

"Oh," I said. "I understand. "Your singing is a way of staying in touch with your relatives. It is like the smartphones that people use."

"No," Harlan explained. "We weren't baying at our families in the Dog Star. We were asking the moon as respectfully as we knew how to please move over so that we might get a better look at the Dog Star. The moon has the annoying habit of blocking our view for a few days each month. We hope that our singing will convince it to do us that one favor. Eventually it will. I am sure of that."

****

Grandma Milly, as I say, is old now. She has difficulty walking. She moves slowly and painfully. Dancing is out of the question, and her sight is not as clear as it used to be. Neither is her hearing. But her mind is sound, and she can still tell good stories to her nieces and nephews and to all the puppies in the neighborhood.

I hadn't seen her for a several weeks and thought I would drop over to say "hi."

It was nighttime. The moon was full. Her neighbor said she wasn't home.

"Where is she?" I asked.

"Oh, she just wandered down the road a bit. She's okay. She took her walker."

I headed off to catch up with her.

There she was, just beyond me in the darkness.

I caught up.

"Hi, Grandma Milly," I said. "Where are you going?"

"I am off to the Dog Star to see my mother," she said cheerfully as she disappeared into the night.

The End

WHERE TRUTH LIES

I am an old guy, a geezer. I have made many notes on my life and my work. I have collected piles of photographs and not a few recordings. I have memories within me both clear and distorted by time. And dreams. Dreams, too, may serve as repositories of the truth.

What to do with all that stuff?

A straightforward narrative is possible. But a danger is tedium. "I did this. I did that." The first person singular shouts dominance. An accountant's memory becomes more a danger than a dreamer's forgetting.

An alternative may simply be to let the mind wander as it will in moments of tedium and peace and to permit the fingers to caress the keyboard freely while what remains of the rational self is engaged in fiction; where the self is released to dance when it must, to wander as in a dream the meaning of which may or may not be determined until long after waking.

Yes. The dream. That is where truth is surely to be found. So it is in religion, in psychotherapy, in art and in literature.

Is not The Tempest an hallucination in which the sorcerer Prospero has evoked a fantasy world of beauty more real than Shakespeare's own? Is one not more awake to sensuality in the magic forest of a Midsummer's Night's Dream than in the tedious real world of royalty?

I am not arguing here of fiction versus fact but rather of a modest loosening of ties to accustomed reality and welcoming instead a mind adrift, not madness so much as relaxing our bodies and our thoughts.

It is in this way that I have authored the Milly stories in which the Wonder Dog and I experience each other not so much as we do in the real world but rather as we draw upon that world to explore who we are or what we may have been and what we might yet be.

In this writing I have asked each story to emerge of its own accord in preparation to the emergence at some later moment of a sliver or two of meaning and even truth.

Or not.